DETROIT LIONS

ALL-TIME GREATS

BY TED COLEMAN

Book design by Jake Slavik
Cover design by Jake Slavik

Photographs ©: Rick Osentoski/AP Images, cover (top), 1 (top); Doug Mills/AP Images, cover (bottom), 1 (bottom); Bettmann/Getty Images, 4, 6, 13; Tim Culek/Getty Images Sport/ Getty Images, 9; Tony Tomsic/Getty Images Sport Classic/Getty Images, 10; Walter Iooss Jr./ Sports Illustrated/Getty Images, 15; Focus on Sport/Getty Images Sport/Getty Images, 16; Al Tielemans/Sports Illustrated/Getty Images, 19; Gregory Shamus/Stringer/Getty Images Sport/ Getty Images, 20

Press Box Books, an imprint of Press Room Editions.

ISBN
978-1-63494-425-0 (library bound)
978-1-63494-442-7 (paperback)
978-1-63494-475-5 (epub)
978-1-63494-459-5 (hosted ebook)

Library of Congress Control Number: 2021916601

Distributed by North Star Editions, Inc.
2297 Waters Drive
Mendota Heights, MN 55120
www.northstareditions.com

Printed in the United States of America
012022

ABOUT THE AUTHOR

Ted Coleman is a sportswriter who lives in Louisville, Kentucky, with his trusty Affenpinscher, Chloe.

TABLE OF CONTENTS

LAYNE
22

CHAPTER 1
THE GOLDEN ERA

The Detroit Lions joined the National Football League (NFL) in 1930. At that time, they were known as the Portsmouth Spartans. Based in southern Ohio, the Spartans were led by tailback **Earl "Dutch" Clark**. Clark was a triple threat. He passed, ran, and even kicked. In 1934, the Spartans moved to Detroit, Michigan, and became the Lions. The next season, Clark led the Lions to an NFL championship.

In 1950, **Bobby Layne** became Detroit's quarterback. Layne had been a star in college. But in his first two NFL seasons, he didn't have much success. That changed when he joined

WALKER
37

the Lions. Layne turned into one of the league's top quarterbacks. He was also a great leader. Teammates loved how hard he competed. Layne led the Lions to three NFL titles in the 1950s.

Layne didn't do it alone, though. Running back **Doak Walker** was there for two of those championship seasons. Walker spent only six years in the NFL. But he made them count. Walker was a strong runner who could also catch passes and kick. He even kicked the winning extra point in the 1953 championship game.

Offensive lineman **Lou Creekmur** made sure Walker had plenty of holes to run through. Creekmur was as tough as they came. He didn't miss a single game for nine

THE CURSE OF BOBBY LAYNE

One year after winning the 1957 NFL title, the Lions traded Bobby Layne to the Pittsburgh Steelers. Layne was unhappy about the trade. He said the Lions wouldn't win another title for 50 years. He turned out to be right. In fact, the team's drought lasted even longer than that. Going into the 2021 season, the Lions had gone 63 years without reaching another championship game.

straight years. He also made the Pro Bowl in eight of his ten seasons.

The Lions weren't just an offensive team. Their defensive backfield was nicknamed "Chris's Crew." Chris referred to safety **Jack Christiansen**. He racked up 46 interceptions during his eight-year career. He was also a great punt returner.

Another key member of the defense was **Joe Schmidt**. He was the captain of the 1957 championship team. Schmidt made a name for himself as a tough middle linebacker. He

CHRISTIANSEN

24

earned a trip to 10 straight Pro Bowls from 1954 to 1963. Schmidt also coached the Lions for a few years in the late 1960s and early 1970s.

LeBEAU
44

CHAPTER 2
THE MIDDLE YEARS

The Lions remained a competitive team into the 1960s. By that point, they were doing it mostly with defense. Defensive back **Yale Lary** had been a key member of Detroit's championship teams of the 1950s. But he was still going strong in the 1960s. Lary wasn't just a great safety, though. He also punted and returned kicks.

Cornerback **Dick LeBeau** was one of the best defensive players of the decade. He could defend runs as well as passes. LeBeau was known as a hard hitter. He also had an eye for the football. His 62 career interceptions are a team record.

Perhaps the most fearsome defensive player in Lions history was **Dick "Night Train" Lane**. The star cornerback was one of the hardest hitters in NFL history. Lane played his last five seasons in Detroit, and they were some of his best years. He made three straight Pro Bowls as a Lion.

Alex Karras was the leader on a tough defensive line. During his 12-year NFL career, he missed only one game due to injury. Karras wasn't the biggest player. But he was quick, and he could chase down the quarterback.

THE FORD FAMILY

Ford is best known for making cars. But the Ford family also owns the Detroit Lions. William Clay Ford Sr. bought the team in 1961 and ran it for more than 50 years. His daughter Sheila Ford Hamp took over as the team's owner in 2020.

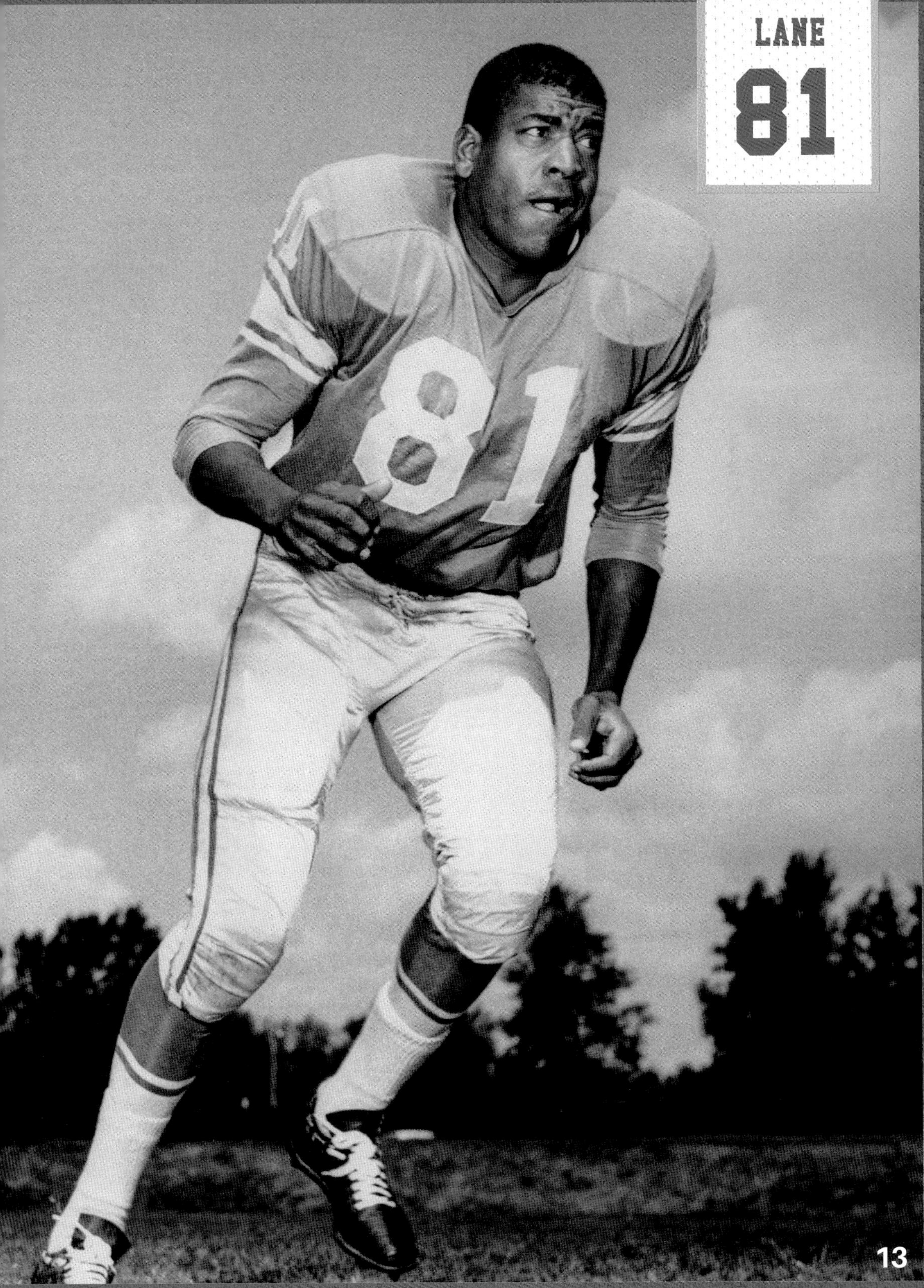

LANE
81

The Lions originally thought **Lem Barney** would be a wide receiver. However, he soon proved to be a great defender. In fact, Barney turned out to be one of the best cornerbacks in team history. He recorded 56 interceptions during his 11 years with Detroit. That put him right behind LeBeau on the team's list of most career interceptions. Barney made the Pro Bowl seven times during his career.

One notable offensive player from this era was tight end **Charlie Sanders**. Sanders played all 10 seasons of his career in Detroit.

STAT SPOTLIGHT

CAREER CATCHES BY A TIGHT END
LIONS TEAM RECORD
Charlie Sanders: 336

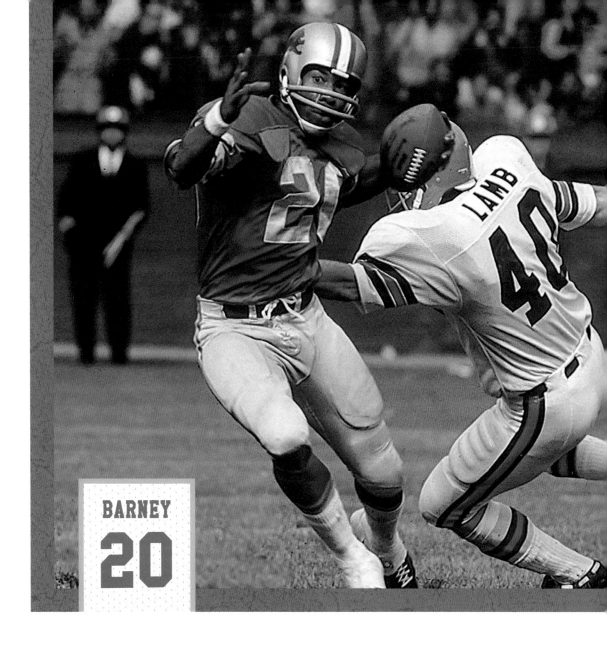

BARNEY
20

He was a great blocker, but he could catch, too.
When he retired after the 1977 season, he had
the most catches in team history.

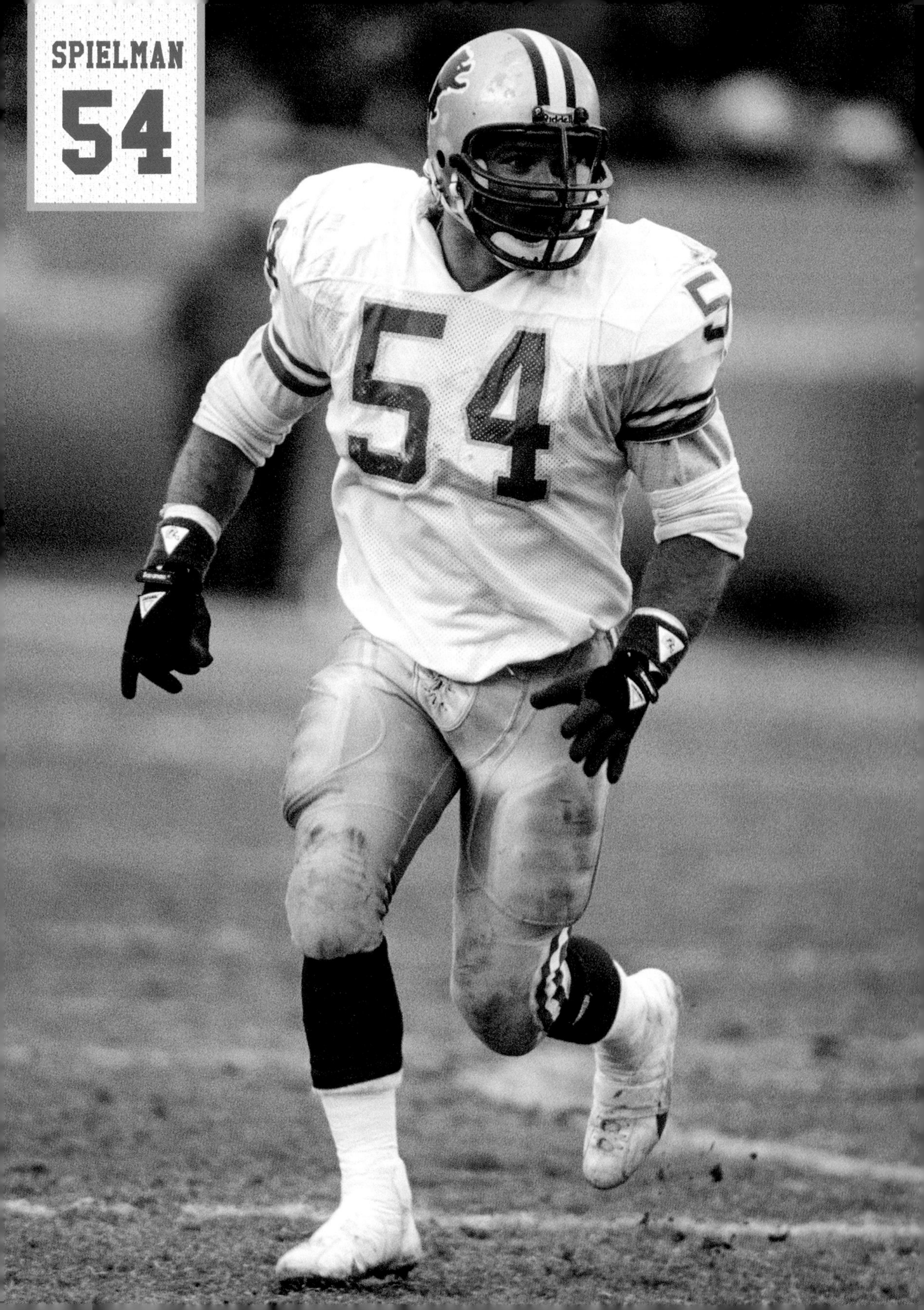
SPIELMAN
54

CHAPTER 3
RESTORING THE ROAR

The Lions struggled in the 1970s. But in the early 1980s, running back **Billy Sims** helped restore their winning ways. Sims led the NFL in touchdowns in his rookie season. He also recorded more than 1,000 yards in three of his first four years. Unfortunately, a knee injury in 1984 ended his promising career.

The Lions reached the playoffs in 1982 and 1983. After that, they struggled again. The team began rebuilding around a defense led by linebacker **Chris Spielman**. Spielman was a team leader and hard worker. He made more tackles than any Lion in history.

In the 1989 draft, the Lions selected running back **Barry Sanders**. He was one of the most exciting players in NFL history. Standing just 5-foot-8, Sanders ran low to the ground and could easily cut past defenders. Sanders made the Pro Bowl in all 10 of his NFL seasons. During that time, he racked up more than 15,000 rushing yards.

Sanders had the help of a great lineman. Left tackle **Lomas Brown** made six straight Pro Bowls as a Lion. Another weapon on offense was wide receiver **Herman Moore**. Moore became the team's all-time leader

QUARTERBACK CONNECTIONS

Matthew Stafford and Bobby Layne are two of the greatest quarterbacks in Lions history. But they share more than just that. They both attended Highland Park High School in Dallas, Texas. Doak Walker went there, too.

SANDERS
20

in catches, yards, and touchdowns. More
importantly, he and Sanders brought winning
back to Detroit.

JOHNSON

81

Wide receiver **Calvin Johnson** joined the Lions in 2007. He ended up breaking all of Moore's major records. His best season was 2012. That year, he set an NFL record for most receiving yards in a season.

Johnson caught most of his passes from quarterback **Matthew Stafford**. Stafford had a powerful arm and great accuracy. He was traded to the Los Angeles Rams after the 2020 season. By that point, he had set all of Detroit's major passing records. As a Lion, he threw for more than 45,000 yards.

Stafford's exit opened the door for the next Lions quarterback. And center **Frank Ragnow** was there to block for him. Ragnow signed a new contract in 2021 that would keep him in Detroit. The team believed he was a leader they could build their future around.

TIMELINE

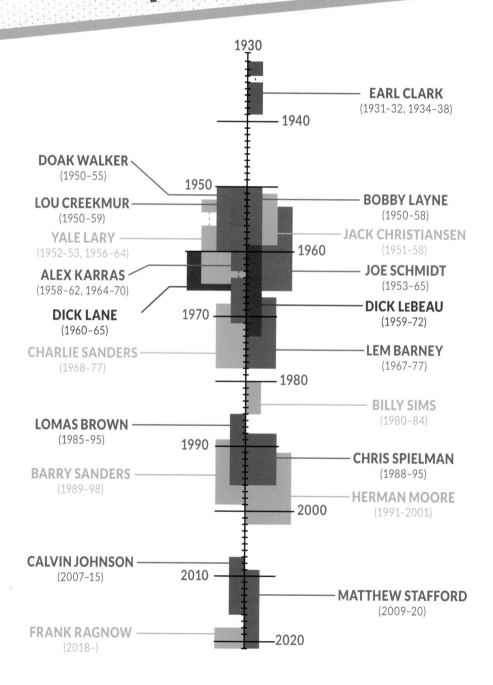

1930

EARL CLARK
(1931–32, 1934–38)

1940

DOAK WALKER
(1950–55)

1950

LOU CREEKMUR
(1950–59)

BOBBY LAYNE
(1950–58)

YALE LARY
(1952–53, 1956–64)

JACK CHRISTIANSEN
(1951–58)

1960

ALEX KARRAS
(1958–62, 1964–70)

JOE SCHMIDT
(1953–65)

DICK LANE
(1960–65)

1970

DICK LeBEAU
(1959–72)

CHARLIE SANDERS
(1968–77)

LEM BARNEY
(1967–77)

1980

BILLY SIMS
(1980–84)

LOMAS BROWN
(1985–95)

1990

CHRIS SPIELMAN
(1988–95)

BARRY SANDERS
(1989–98)

HERMAN MOORE
(1991–2001)

2000

CALVIN JOHNSON
(2007–15)

2010

MATTHEW STAFFORD
(2009–20)

FRANK RAGNOW
(2018–)

2020

DETROIT LIONS

Team history: Portsmouth Spartans (1930–33), Detroit Lions (1934–)

NFL championships: 4 (1935, 1952, 1953, 1957)

Super Bowl titles: 0*

Key coaches:

Potsy Clark (1931-40), 53-25-7,
1 NFL championship

Buddy Parker (1951-56), 47-23-2,
2 NFL championships

Wayne Fontes (1988-96), 66-67-0

MORE INFORMATION

To learn more about the Detroit Lions, go to **pressboxbooks.com/AllAccess**.

These links are routinely monitored and updated to provide the most current information available.

*1966 through 2020

GLOSSARY

cornerback
A defensive player who covers wide receivers near the sidelines.

draft
An event that allows teams to choose new players coming into the league.

linebacker
A player who lines up behind the defensive linemen and in front of the defensive backs.

playoffs
A set of games to decide a league's champion.

rookie
A professional athlete in his or her first year of competition.

safety
A defensive player who covers wide receivers in the middle of the field.

INDEX